The Little Mermaid

H.C.Andersen 🐟 Lisbeth Zwerger

a mini-minedition book

English edition published 2015 by Michael Neugebauer Publishing Ltd., Hong Kong
Distributed in Northa America by IPG, Chicago

Illustrations copyright © 2004 by Lisbeth Zwerger
First published in 2000 by Michael Neugebauer Verlag AG, Zurich, Switzerland.
Rights arranged with "minedition" Rights and Licensing AG, Zurich, Switzerland.
Michael Neugebauer Publishing Ltd., Unit 23, 7F, Kowloon Bay Industrial Centre,
15 Wang Hoi Road, Kowloon Bay, Hong Kong. e-mail: info@minedition.com
This book was printed in April 2015 at L.Rex Printing Co Ltd 3/F., Blue Box Factory
Building, 25 Hing Wo Street, Tin Wan, Aberdeen, Hong Kong, China
Typesetting in New Veljovic Book / ExPonMM
Library of Congress Cataloging-in-Publication Data available upon request.

ISBN 978-988-8240-97-5

10 9 8 7 6 5 4 3 2 1
First impression

For more information please visit our website: www.minedition.com

The Little Mermaid

by H.C.Andersen
Pictures by Lisbeth Zwerger

Translated and retold by
Anthea Bell

minedition

$\mathcal{F}$ar out at sea, where the water is clear but very deep, the merfolk live. Strange trees and plants grow on the sea bed, fish swim among them, and the sea king's castle with its coral walls and amber windows lies in the deepest place of all.

The sea king was a widower, and his old mother kept house for him. She loved her six granddaughters, the little sea princesses. They were all pretty, but the youngest was the loveliest of all. Her skin was like a rose petal, her eyes were blue, but like all the merfolk she had a fishtail instead of legs.

The princesses played all day long in the castle and the garden outside it, where trees of fiery red and dark blue bore shining golden fruit. Each little princess had her own small garden plot to care for.

One of the gardens was shaped like a whale, another like a little mermaid, but the youngest princess made hers as round as the sun. She was a quiet, dreamy child, and she wanted nothing in her garden but rose-red flowers, and the statue of a beautiful boy which had been washed down from a shipwreck to the bottom of the sea.

The little mermaid loved to hear tales of the human world above, and made her old grandmother tell her all she knew about it.

"When you are fifteen," their grandmother told the mermaids, "you will be allowed to come up out of the sea, sit on the rocks in the moonlight, watch the ships sailing by, and see forests and cities from afar!"

Next year the eldest sister would be fifteen, but the youngest still had five years to wait. At night she stood at her window looking up through the dark blue water where the fish swam. And if a black shape moved among them she knew it was either a whale overhead or a ship full of human beings.

On the eldest princess's fifteenth birthday she went up above the surface of the sea. She had many tales to tell when she came home, but best of all, she said, had been lying on a sandbank by moonlight, looking at the great city on the coast nearby.

Next year the second sister came up out of the water on her birthday. She surfaced just as the sun was setting, and she thought the sunset the most beautiful thing she had ever seen. The whole sky had looked like gold, she said.

The year after that it was the third sister's turn. She boldly swam up a broad river that flowed into the sea. She saw beautiful green hills, she heard birds singing, and in a little bay she met a crowd of small human children splashing in the water.

The fourth sister was not so daring, and stayed out among the wild waves. You could see for many miles there, she said, and the sky was like a great glass bell above the sea. She had seen ships far away, looking like seagulls.

Next it was the fifth sister's turn. Her birthday was in winter, so she saw glittering icebergs floating on the green sea. She climbed on one of the biggest and let her long hair blow in the wind. Then a storm came, and there was fear and terror aboard the ships cruising round the iceberg, while the fifth mermaid watched lightning flash above the shining sea.

In the evenings, when storms rose and the five sisters knew that ships would capsize, they swam ahead of them, singing wonderful songs of the beautiful sights to be seen on the sea bed. But the sailors were drowned by the time they reached the sea king's castle.

When her elder sisters rose through the water arm in arm, their little sister felt she would weep, but mermaids cannot shed tears. "Oh, if only I were fifteen!" she said. "I know I shall love the world up above and the people who live there!"

At last her fifteenth birthday came.

"There, now you're off our hands," said her grandmother. And she put a wreath of white lilies in her hair.

The sun had just set when she raised her head above the surface, but the evening star shone brightly. The air was fresh and mild, the sea was calm. There lay a great ship with three masts, and the sailors were all on deck.

The little mermaid swam up to a porthole. She looked through it, and saw a great many finely dressed people. The most handsome of all was a young prince, and this was his birthday. When he stepped out on deck rockets shot into the air. The ship itself was brightly lit, and music played.

It grew late, but the little mermaid couldn't take her eyes off the ship and the handsome prince. Then the waves rose, huge clouds came up, and lightning flashed in the distance. A terrible storm was coming, and the sailors reefed the sails.

The ship creaked and groaned, the water rose like black mountains, the mainmast snapped and the vessel tipped over.

In a flash of lightning, the little mermaid looked around for the young prince, and just as the ship split in two she saw him fall into the sea. Human beings, she knew, cannot live in water – oh, he mustn't die! She swam deep down until at last she found him. He would certainly have drowned if the little mermaid hadn't reached him, for his eyes were closing, but she kept his head above water, and they both drifted with the waves.

In the morning the storm was over, but the ship had sunk. The prince's eyes were still closed. The mermaid kissed his beautiful brow and stroked back his wet hair, willing him to live. At last she swam ashore with him in a little bay and laid him down on the beach in the sun.

There was a large white building in a garden beyond the bay, and now bells rang inside it and some girls came out into the garden. The little mermaid swam away and hid behind tall rocks, waiting to see who would find the poor prince.

Before long a girl saw him and fetched other people, and the mermaid saw the prince revive and smile at them. But he never looked out to sea to smile at her; after all, he didn't know that she had saved him. She felt very sad as she returned to her father's castle.

After that she often came up from the sea where she had left the prince. But she never saw him again, so she went home even sadder than before. In the end she could bear it no longer, and told her sisters her story. A friend of one of the mermaids knew who the prince was; she had seen the birthday party on board the ship herself, and she knew where his kingdom lay.

"Come along, little sister!" said the other princesses, and they all rose from the sea where the prince's castle stood. It was built of pale yellow stone, with gilded domes, and a flight of marble steps went straight down to the sea.

Now the little mermaid knew where the prince lived, and she often swam to the castle again. She sometimes went close enough to gaze at the young prince on his balcony, or she peeped through the green reeds and saw him out sailing in his fine boat.

She longed to come up out of the water and live in the human world herself. "If human beings don't happen to drown," she asked her grandmother, "can they live for ever? Don't they die as we do here under the sea?"

"Yes," said her grandmother, "they die too, even sooner than we do. We can live for three hundred years, but then we turn into foam on the sea. We have no immortal souls, like humans, who rise to the shining stars after death!"

"Is there no way I can win an immortal soul?" asked the little mermaid sadly.

"No!" said the old lady. "Not unless a man loved you enough to be yours for all eternity. But up on earth they think your fishtail is ugly, and only what they call legs are beautiful! So let us be happy and enjoy our three hundred years of life. There's going to be a court ball this evening."

It was a magnificent ball. But still the little mermaid could not forget the handsome prince. "I will venture anything to win the man I love and an immortal soul!" she thought. "I'll visit the sea witch. Perhaps she can help me!"

No flowers grew near the witch's dwelling. There was only the bare, sandy sea floor where turbulent water swirled.

The little mermaid almost turned back, but then she thought of the prince and of a human soul, and she went on until she came to a place where big, fat sea serpents coiled. A house built from the white bones of shipwrecked mariners stood here, and the sea witch sat inside it.

"I know what you want," the sea witch told the mermaid. "It's a stupid wish, but you shall have it, for it will bring you bad luck. If you swim to land before sunrise, sit on the shore and drink the potion I'll give you, your tail will fall off and turn into legs. You'll be as graceful as ever, but every step you take will hurt like sharp knives. Will you suffer all this?"

"Yes!" said the little mermaid, thinking of the prince.

"Remember," said the witch, "if you don't win the prince's love, you will never get an immortal soul! On the morning after he marries another your heart will break and you will be foam on the sea."

"And you must pay me too," said the witch, "You must give me your sweet voice in payment for my precious potion! Put out your tongue for me to cut it off."

"Very well," said the little mermaid, and the witch put her cauldron on to boil. At last the potion was ready, and looked like the clearest water!

The mermaid swam to the prince's castle in the bright moonlight and drank the potion. It hurt so much that she fainted away. At sunrise she woke to find that her fishtail was gone and she had legs instead. The handsome prince was standing before her. When he asked who she was, she looked at him gently yet very sadly, for she could not speak. Then he took her hand and led her into the castle. Every step felt like treading on sharp knives, but she bore it gladly.

Everyone in the castle was enchanted by her, especially the prince, who said she must stay with him always. He took her out with him riding or climbing mountains, and although her feet bled she just laughed and followed him. Back in the castle, she went out to the marble steps by night. The cold sea water cooled her burning feet, and then she thought of the merfolk down beneath the waves.
One night her sisters came up arm in arm, singing sadly, and told her how they grieved for her.

Day by day she became dearer to the prince, but it never entered his head to marry her. "You remind me of a girl I once saw when I was shipwrecked near a temple," said the prince. "She saved my life. She is the only woman in the world I could ever love!"

But now the prince was to sail away in a fine ship and be married to a king's daughter. "I must see this princess, but I cannot love her!" he told the mermaid. "If I were ever to choose a bride it would be you!" And she dreamed of human happiness and an immortal soul as she sat by the ship's rail and looked down through the clear water. Her sisters came up, wringing their white hands, and she waved to them and smiled.

Next morning the ship came to the foreign king's city. The bells rang and there were parties every day, and the princess, who had been brought up far away in a temple, came home at last.

"It is you!" said the prince. "You rescued me when I was left for dead on the sea shore!" And he clasped her to his breast. But the little mermaid felt as if her heart would break, for when he married she would die and become foam on the sea.

All the bells rang for the wedding, and the little mermaid carried the bride's train, thinking sadly of all she had lost. That evening they boarded the prince's ship.

The sails swelled in the wind, and the sailors danced on deck. The little mermaid danced too, and her tender feet hurt, but the pain in her heart was sharper still.

She knew that she would never see the prince again, or the deep sea and the sky bright with stars. Eternal night awaited her, for she had no soul.

At last the prince and his bride went to their tent. All was still on deck. The little mermaid looked east; she knew that the first ray of the sun would kill her. Then she saw her sisters come up out of the sea. They were pale, and their beautiful long hair had all been cut off.

"We sold it to the witch!" they called. "She gave us a sharp knife to save you – here it is! Before the sun rises you must drive it into the prince's heart, and when his warm blood splashes on your feet they will turn back into a fishtail, and you will be a mermaid again. Hurry! Either he or you must die before the sun rises!"

Then they sighed and sank into the waves.

The little mermaid looked inside the tent, saw the bride resting with her head on the prince's breast, and she bent down to kiss him, looked up at the sky, looked at the sharp knife, and then she threw it far out to sea. As her sight failed, she flung herself off the ship too, and felt her body dissolve into foam.

The sun rose above the waves, yet the little mermaid did not feel as if she were dying. She saw hundreds of beautiful, translucent creatures hovering above her. Their voices were melodious, their lightness carried them up through the air without wings. The little mermaid saw that she too had a body like theirs and was rising from the foam.

"Where am I going?" she asked.

"To join the daughters of the air!" they replied. "Like mermaids, we have no immortal souls, but we can win one by doing good deeds. We are flying to the hot countries to bring refreshment and healing to the sick. When we have done all the good we can for three hundred years we will be granted immortal souls. You have tried to do good too, poor little mermaid, and now you can win a soul yourself."

Then the little mermaid raised her bright arms to the sun, and for the first time she could shed tears. Down on the ship, she saw the prince and his bride. Unseen, she smiled at the prince, and with the other children of the air she rose to the clouds sailing through the sky.

"In three hundred years' time we shall fly like this into the kingdom of God!" she said.

Most recent books illustrated by LISBETH ZWERGER
and published by minedition:

TALES FROM THE BROTHERS GRIMM
ISBN 978-988-8240-53-1

THE PIED PIPER OF HAMELIN
A Legend by the Brothers Grimm
ISBN 978-988-8240-82-1

THE NIGHT BEFORE CHRISTMAS
ISBN 978-988-8240-88-3

THE SELFISH GIANT
ISBN 978-988-8240-99-9

For more information please visit our website: www.minedition.com